W9-AUO-695

Valentine Frankenstein

Other Little Apple Paperbacks
you will enjoy:

Teeth Week
by Nancy Alberts

Vampires Don't Wear Polka Dots
by Debra Dadey and Marcia Jones

The Neighbor from Outer Space
by Maureen George

Rent a Third Grader
by B.B. Hiller

Sarah with an H
by Elaine Moore

Valentine Frankenstein

By Maggie Twohill

SCHOLASTIC INC.
New York Toronto London Auckland Sydney

If you purchased this book without a cover, you should be aware that this book is stolen property. It was reported as "unsold and destroyed" to the publisher, and neither the author nor the publisher has received any payment for this "stripped book."

No part of this publication may be reproduced in whole or in part, or stored in a retrieval system, or transmitted in any form or by any means, electronic, mechanical, photocopying, recording, or otherwise, without written permission of the publisher. For information regarding permission, write to Bradbury Press, an affiliate of Macmillan, Inc., a division of Macmillan Publishing Company, 866 Third Avenue, New York, NY 10022.

ISBN 0-590-46039-0

Copyright © 1991 by Maggie Twohill. All rights reserved. Published by Scholastic Inc., 730 Broadway, New York, NY 10003, by arrangement with Bradbury Press, an affiliate of Macmillan, Inc. APPLE PAPERBACKS is a registered trademark of Scholastic Inc.

12 11 10 9 8 8 9/9

Printed in the U.S.A. 40

First Scholastic printing, January 1994

For a fine young designer-director,
Braden LuBell

Contents

1

Valentine Vote

Amanda Pinkerton stared hard into the mirror over the bathroom sink.

She placed the knuckle of her index finger under the tip of her nose and pushed up. She turned her head to the right, then to the left.

She opened her eyes wider and leaned right into the mirror for a super close-up.

"Amanda!" her mother called from downstairs.

"I'll be right there!"

"You're going to be late for school!"

"No, I won't—"

"I can already see Walter coming toward here. He'll be at the door any minute!"

Amanda sighed. Walter was *always* at the door ten minutes earlier than necessary.

Her mother had left a stick of lip gloss on the counter and Amanda tried some on. She smiled at herself in the mirror and then tried the upturned nose effect again.

"A-*man*-da!"

"Mom, I'll be right there!"

Amanda gave the mirror a quick wave and hurried downstairs, grabbing her books from the hall table on her way.

"I put some bananas in your cereal," her mother said, setting a bowl down at Amanda's place at the table.

"Thanks—"

"If you got down here earlier in the mornings you could get a ride with your dad." Mrs. Pinkerton said this every morning.

"I know, Mom."

"Jackie Sue gets a ride every day." Jackie Sue was Amanda's younger sister.

"I like to walk, Mom. It's healthier than riding in an overheated car. You should walk, too. And I'm never late."

"Walter's here," Mrs. Pinkerton said, and opened the kitchen door.

Walter Brinkman was Amanda's neighbor. Both the Pinkertons and the Brinkmans had moved to Daisy Lane at the same time. Walter and Amanda were the same age. They had gone to play school, day camp, and elementary school together. Walter had always called for Amanda every morning for school and still did, even though they were in the fifth grade now and pretty grown up.

Amanda didn't mind. Walter was her oldest friend. She liked him, even though some of the girls at school teased her about him. They sometimes made fun of Walter, which bothered Amanda, and she said so.

Now he was standing over her, watching her eat Rice Krispies with bananas.

"Hi, Amanda," he offered timidly, and stuck a finger into the collar of his parka to loosen it.

"Hm, Wltr," Amanda mumbled, chewing.

Walter shifted from one foot to another. "It's cold out," he said.

"Mmm," Amanda grunted.

"Well . . . it's supposed to be . . . it's winter," Walter said. And then he honked. Amanda's friend Karen called it "Walter's honk," but it was more of a snort. Amanda, defending him, said it was the way Walter laughed, inhaling through his nose, that made the sound, which resembled an *ohhnk, ohhnk.* It made the other kids snicker and giggle, so Walter tried hard not to honk in front of them. But Amanda was different.

Amanda slurped up the last of the cereal and looked at the spoon. It was sticky from the lip gloss she had forgotten to blot.

"Ready?" Walter asked eagerly.

"Amanda, wear your scarf," her mother cautioned.

"Okay." She began to load herself into all the outerwear required for winters in upstate New York. "Let's go, Walter," she said.

"Here's your lunch." Her mother handed her a brown paper bag.

"Thanks—"

"Don't forget your books, Amanda," Walter said, scooping them up.

"I won't forget them, Walter," Amanda said.

"Wow, it *is* cold," Amanda said, pulling the scarf tighter around her neck.

"Told you."

They headed down the block, crunching snow under their shoes. The snow wasn't fresh, but it tended to stick around for a long time.

Walter sniffled. "Did you do that book report? The biography?" he asked.

"Yeah. I did Mike Tyson."

"*Mike Tyson?* You did *Mike Tyson?*"

"Yeah, Walter, I did Mike Tyson."

"You're not supposed to do sports people—"

"Who said? Mrs. Tragg just said 'biography.' "

Walter scratched his head with his mittened fingers. "I did Martin Luther King."

"Well . . . that's okay, too."

"Come on, Amanda, he was *important*!"

Amanda looked at him. "Mrs. Tragg didn't say the subject had to be *important,* Walter."

They walked on in silence for a while.

"Only one more year and we'll be in junior high," Walter said, looking at the overcast sky.

"Mmm, that'll be great."

"Yeah. I bet I'll be different in junior high."

Amanda tilted her head toward him. "Different? How?"

"Oh—I dunno. Just . . . different. There'll be a lot more kids in our class, you know, from the other elementary schools . . . so I'll have some new people to be with."

Amanda thought about that.

"You don't like the kids we're with now?" she asked. But she thought she knew the answer. Walter didn't have as many friends as she had. In fact . . . Amanda frowned . . . he really didn't have . . . uh . . .

"Some," Walter said quickly. "I like some. But I think I'll do better in a different environment."

Amanda wasn't sure about that. Walter would still be Walter, no matter what the environment, she thought. He'd still honk through his nose and he'd still wear that look on his face that announced to the world that if he were a puppy, he'd be the last one to be picked out of the whole kennel. At least he always got good grades, but that didn't seem to help. Amanda smiled at him to make him feel better, anyway.

They reached the Barker Goodhue Elementary School (named after a long-dead wealthy man who had donated a lot of money to their town) just as the next-to-last bell was ringing and everyone was hurrying inside.

"Bye, Walter," Amanda called, as she ran toward the door. But she didn't wait for his answer. She had seen two of her girlfriends waving and holding the door open for her.

"Hi, Karen!" Amanda called, bouncing up the stairs. "Hi, Jen!"

"Hi, Amanda. Don't you want to wait for your boyfriend?" Karen teased.

Amanda made a bored face.

"Ohhnk, ohhnk," Karen snorted and Jen giggled.

"Stop. Walter's really nice. You shouldn't be so mean," Amanda said.

"Oh, I know Walter's not bad," Karen said, "he's just so . . . so . . ."

"He's a stick," Jen said. "He's just like a stick. You know, straight and boring and no fun. And he always looks like he should be wearing one of those signs on his back that says Kick Me."

"Stop, I mean it. I wouldn't let anyone say anything bad about you two, so don't say anything bad about Walter. He's my friend, too. Anyway . . . Walter can be fun." She looked at their faces. "He can!" she insisted. "Uh-oh, there's the last bell—"

They all hurried to their homeroom.

Melissa Goobitz was the president of Amanda's fifth-grade class. Melissa didn't do very much as president except remind everyone in the class that she *was* president and to have her parents remind all their relatives and friends about it, too. The office of president of Mrs. Tragg's fifth grade class was really an honorary position, but it taught the class something about the election process and how it worked. Occasionally,

Melissa presided over a homeroom meeting, and she always got to choose which person would lead the Pledge of Allegiance each morning.

Now today, as Melissa stood at the front of the room, smugly surveying the class to find someone deserving of the honor she was about to bestow, Karen and Amanda cringed.

"She wants press conferences, like the real president," Karen whispered. "She wants to be on TV and have big dinner parties with other class presidents. She wants a helicopter to fly her to camp . . . and Europe and stuff."

"Yeah," Amanda sighed, "but we elected her. We can't complain."

"*I* can complain. I didn't vote for her. And neither did you."

Amanda giggled. "Everyone in the whole class says they didn't vote for Melissa, so how did she get to be president, anyhow?"

"I think she wrote out a whole lot of

extra ballots with her name on them and put them in the box herself. Remember what Mrs. Tragg taught us? It's called 'stuffing the ballot box.' Only they can't do that today too easily because they've got computerized—"

"Karen!"

Karen jumped and sat up straight. "Huh?"

Melissa was pointing to her. "I pick *you,*" she said.

"For the *Pledge,*" Amanda whispered, and poked Karen's arm.

"Ohh!" Karen stood and made her way up to the front.

"Aren't you going to say 'thank you'?" Melissa hissed at her as she went by.

Karen dipped into a curtsy and the class laughed.

Usually after the Pledge of Allegiance, their first subject for the day was English. Amanda was opening her notebook to her book report when Mrs.

Tragg tapped her pencil on her desk.

"Before we get to our reports, boys and girls, Melissa has something she'd like to discuss with you. Melissa?"

Someone in the back of the room groaned, but Melissa ignored it. She folded her hands together and smiled at her classmates.

"Well, you all know that next Tuesday is Valentine's Day, right?"

"We know, we know." Karen sighed. "She already pushed through a valentine dance for next week. What does she want us to do now, dress up as hearts for it?"

"I forgot about that dance," Amanda said. "It's Friday, isn't it?"

"Yeah, we couldn't get the gym on Tuesday. Sounds so exciting, I can't wait, can you?" Karen yawned.

"And I was thinking that we ought to reinstate the custom of a class valentine box," Melissa continued.

"A what?" someone asked.

Jen leaned over her desk and tapped Amanda. "*Valentine* box?" she asked.

"The last time we had one was in third grade," Melissa went on. "We all made it in art, remember? Everyone cut out hearts and things and we pasted them on this big box and then we all brought in valentine cards for our friends? Remember?"

"No," one of the boys said.

"Yes, you do. It was fun. It should be a tradition, I think. It's an old-fashioned holiday celebrated in an old-fashioned way. I think we should do it again. We should have the box *and* we should bring valentines to put in it."

"Wait a minute," Karen said. "We're having a valentine dance. Doesn't that take care of the tradition idea?"

Melissa frowned. "A valentine box is fun," she insisted.

"Oh, it's okay when you're in third grade, Melissa, but don't you think we're a little old for it now?"

"No!"

"The only people who like valentine boxes are people who get a lot of valentines," Jen said. "What makes Melissa think she's going to get a lot of them?"

Karen giggled. "The same thing that made her get elected president—she'll write them herself!"

"Karen . . ." Amanda said chidingly, but she smiled.

"Let's take a vote," one of the boys called out. "See how the class feels about it right now."

"No, no," Melissa said quickly. "We're going to do it the way they do in the United States Senate." She nodded smugly for emphasis. "We're going to have a discussion about it."

In the back, someone groaned.

"She always gets her way." Laura Leff sighed.

A boy named Buddy, sitting to Amanda's left, tapped her on the shoulder. When she turned to face him, he handed her a slip of paper.

"Note," he said, indicating someone from the back had passed it to him.

Amanda unfolded it. "Vote *no*! *Please,* Amanda! Make everyone vote *no*!" the note read.

Amanda turned around. From the back row near the closets, Walter was signaling frantically to her.

NO, he was mouthing. Vote *no-o-ooo*!

"I do remember valentine boxes," Caroline Burke was saying. "They *were* kind of fun. You never put your name on the valentine. You always sent it anonymously to someone you really liked, and then he or she had to guess who sent it."

"And," Melissa added, "if that person likes you back, then—"

"Then, what?" Karen wanted to know.

"*Then* you could get to know each other better! Which you never would have done if someone hadn't sent the card!"

"It's babyish," Jen said.

Kenny Eckhart agreed. "Forget it," he said.

Melissa folded her arms and planted her feet firmly in front of her. "We have the valentine dance next Friday, but we don't have anything special on Tuesday, which is the real holiday. If we have the valentine box, then we *won't* have last period social studies."

Kenny said, "Huh?"

"No social studies? But we're having a quiz," Jen said.

Melissa looked over at the teacher. "Mrs. Tragg said if we voted to have a valentine box, then we could have a party. We'd have the quiz the next Monday instead. Then we'd have the whole weekend to study for it. Want to have a vote now?" She grinned at them.

"Yeah! Vote!" Donny Greenfield yelled.

Amanda turned around to look at Walter. His face had crumpled.

Poor Walter, she thought. He's worried because he thinks he'll be the only one in the class who won't get any valentines. She glanced around the room. Mmmm, he could be right, too. . . .

Melissa called for a vote. All the hands but Walter's were in the air. Even Karen voted yes.

2
Poor Walter

"I think I spoke too soon." Jen sighed as she and Amanda and Karen walked toward the art room. "All I was thinking about was getting out of a social studies quiz, but now I have to think about valentines. Do we actually have to *send* one?"

"It doesn't matter," Karen said with a shrug. "You don't have to put your name on it, so go for it! I mean, think about the person you really like. . . ." She grinned slyly.

"I don't really like any boy in our class," Amanda said.

"Oh, come on, Amanda. You always said Kenny was cute."

"Kenny Eckhart?"

"Amanda, there's only one Kenny in the whole fifth grade."

In spite of herself, Amanda blushed. "I'd feel stupid sending a valentine card to Kenny Eckhart. Anyway, he'll probably get one from every girl in the class. What about you two? Who'll you be sending valentines to?"

Jen and Karen looked at each other. "I don't know," Jen said, making a face.

"Me neither." Karen sighed. "Why don't we just send them to our girlfriends like we did in the third grade? That way we can at least be assured of getting one."

"I sent one to Mark Smith in the third grade," Jen said.

"You did?" Amanda asked. "What did you sign it?"

"Oh, I was very original," Jen replied. "I signed it 'Guess Who?' Of course, he did."

"He did? He guessed? How?"

"Because when he opened it, he looked all around the class and I was the only one looking right back at him with a face as red as the stripes on the flag. And when he saw me and his jaw dropped about a mile, I burst into the most hysterical fit of giggling I ever had. I have never been more embarrassed in my whole life. I can't believe you two don't remember it."

"I don't remember it," Amanda said. "And I don't remember your ever telling us about it, either."

They reached the art room and took seats at their work tables. The art teacher was a tall, redheaded woman named Ms. Simms, who was very fond of abstract art and encouraged freedom of expression in her students. When they had painted self-portraits back in October, she framed and hung the ones that looked least like their models. Amanda's portrait resembled squares and circles inside a pentagon, and Ms. Simms gave it a place of honor.

"Class, I understand you're to have a valentine party next Tuesday."

"How did she find out so soon?" Jen asked. "We just voted!"

"Melissa probably told her last week," Karen said.

"So, today I think we'll use the period to make the valentine box and some decorations for the dance."

There was a little groan from the back. Amanda recognized it. She turned around, but Walter had his face buried in his arm on the desk, so she couldn't give him an encouraging smile.

"I guess we should make hearts, huh?" Laura asked.

"Well, the heart has always been a symbol of Valentine's Day, that's true," Ms. Simms agreed, "but let's see what original ideas you can come up with."

"That means," Karen said, "cut out green and black rectangular hearts."

Amanda giggled.

Amanda didn't walk home with Walter that afternoon, but they often didn't end the school day together. Walter had piano lessons on Mondays and allergy shots on Tuesdays. Amanda had tap on Tuesdays and Girl Scouts on Wednesdays.

Today was Thursday and neither of them had any after-school activity, but somehow they missed each other after the final bell rang.

Amanda's head was full of thoughts of the upcoming valentine dance. She thought she liked the way she looked in her mother's lip gloss and she definitely liked the way her nose looked when she turned it up with her knuckle, even though Karen had burst out laughing when she showed her. Kenny Eckhart.

Mmm . . . She wondered if she should send him a valentine on Tuesday. Maybe he wouldn't get that many and he might figure out that she was the one who'd sent it and if he did, maybe—just maybe—he might ask her to dance.

She was about a block from her house when she heard it. A faint shuffling sound, coming from somewhere behind her. She turned and spotted Walter. His head was down, but she knew that *he* knew she was there. She slowed her walk, but he slowed his, too.

Amanda sighed. Poor Walter, she thought. He's probably thinking about Valentine's Day, too. She remembered his horrified face when Melissa had called for the vote about the valentine box.

Finally, she just stopped walking and Walter caught up.

"Why didn't you say something?" Amanda asked him. "You were right there behind me."

"I'm not feeling very cheerful," he told her. "I didn't want to put you in a bad mood, too."

"You won't put me in a bad mood. What's the matter?" Amanda asked, though she knew.

"I've been thinking about next Tuesday. I mean—I know I'm not the best-looking, most popular boy at Goodhue, but it's worse when you have your nose rubbed in it, you know what I mean?"

"I think so. You're worried you won't get any valentines and everyone else will and you'll be embarrassed. Is that it?"

"Humiliated is more the word," Walter said. "I only got one valentine back in the third grade and that was from you, Amanda."

"So?" She bristled. "What's so bad about that?"

"Oh, no, you know what I mean! We're *friends.* I mean friends are different from—you know. I mean—I mean—"

"What do you mean, Walter?"

"I mean if we weren't friends, you never would have sent me a card. Would you?"

"Walter," Amanda said, "I'm ten-and-a-half years old. Friends are about all I can handle right now. It's very nice to have friends."

"I know, Amanda. But you're my only real friend."

Amanda felt a lump rise in her throat. His only real friend! How awful! How would she feel if she were Walter? He sounded so miserable he made her want to cry.

How could she make Walter feel better? How could she make more people like him?

Well, she couldn't do that. You can't make people like someone.

"Listen, Walter," she said, "you really are a terrific person."

"You think so?"

"Yeah."

"Why?"

"Why?"

"Yeah, Amanda. Why am I terrific?"

Amanda swallowed. "Well," she said.

Walter ducked his head. "See?" he said. "You can't think of any reason."

Amanda thought hard. "You're a good friend," she said. "And you're very smart. And . . . you're nice to animals. And whenever I'm sick, you always bring my homework over right away. . . ."

"Aw, Amanda . . ."

"No, Walter, the things I'm talking about may not be all that exciting. I mean you wouldn't see them as the headlines in the morning paper or anything, but—but they're important. I mean . . . they're important to me. You're nice and you're a good friend."

"Thanks." Walter sighed. "You're a good friend, too."

Amanda looked at him. "Do you think I'm terrific?" she asked.

He blushed. "Well . . . sure . . ."

"Well, okay. I like you and I'm terrific, so would I like someone who wasn't terrific, too?" That was pretty good logic, Amanda thought.

Walter thought about it.

"But . . . why are you the *only* terrific person who thinks I'm terrific?" he asked.

They had reached Amanda's front walk. "Listen, Walter," she said, heading for her porch, "don't worry about it, okay? My dad has a saying, he says it all the time. It goes like this: 'Ninety-nine percent of the things you worry about never, never happen.' Just remember that, okay, Walter?"

"Well, okay," he called back. "But, hey, Amanda, what about that one percent, huh? *Ohhnk, ohhnk!*"

But Amanda had just closed the front door behind her.

3

Amanda's Experiment

"Amanda, is that you?" her mother called.

"Uh-huh."

"Good, because I want you to take care of the laundry downstairs, okay?"

"Okay."

"And then I want you to help Jackie Sue with her project."

"What project?"

"I'm not sure, but she needs something from the store to finish it."

"Okay."

"Was that Walter I just saw leaving?"

"Yeah."

"Why didn't you invite him in?"

Amanda leaned against the hall table. She scratched her head just above her left ear.

Mom likes Walter, she thought. *I* like Walter. So how come nobody else seems to like Walter? That's what he wanted to know and I couldn't answer it. I just told him Daddy's favorite saying about ninety-nine percent of the things you worry about.

She walked slowly toward the kitchen where her mom was writing letters. Amanda's mom taught morning nursery school, so she was usually home by the time Amanda and Jackie Sue were out of school.

"Mom?" she said.

"Mmm . . ."

"You like Walter Brinkman, don't you?"

Mrs. Pinkerton looked up. "Of course I do, Amanda. Don't you?"

"Oh, yeah . . . I do . . . but how come

no one else seems to like him?"

"Who? Do you mean Karen? And Jennifer?"

"Well, not just Karen and Jen. The boys, too. I mean, at lunch time, he always sits by himself, never with the other kids. And sometimes I get teased for being his friend."

Mrs. Pinkerton frowned. "I'm sorry about that. His mother worries about him, too. He's a very smart boy and sweet. . . ."

Amanda nodded. When they were little, Walter knew all about how to build the best sand castles. He knew how to make mobiles with Play-Doh and paper, and he always knew how to do the math in every class from first grade on. And as they grew older, he would tell Amanda what was new in the news and what professional teams would probably win their games and why. And he knew more about music than almost anyone Amanda could imagine.

"So how come he has hardly any friends?" Amanda asked again.

Mrs. Pinkerton put down her pen and thought for a moment. "It probably has to do with the way he approaches people."

"Huh?"

"Well, you know, when you see your friends at school every day, what do you do?"

"Uh—wave and say hi and then run and catch up. Why?"

"What does Walter do?"

Now Amanda frowned. "Well . . . he kind of . . . drops his head . . . like this . . . and he kind of . . . doesn't look at anybody."

Mrs. Pinkerton took a deep breath and then let it out. "Okay," she said. "Now if you were another kid, what kind of message would you get from that?"

"That Walter's probably very shy," Amanda answered.

"Yes . . . shy . . . and that perhaps he's

someone with very little confidence in himself, right?"

"Oh, right," Amanda agreed. "But if you're smart and nice, why wouldn't you have any confidence?"

"Everyone's different, Amanda, I can't explain that. But youngsters who hang back from the group and tend to keep to themselves usually aren't the ones the other children will seek out."

Amanda thought that over. "I guess," she said. "But Walter kind of snorts at you, too, did you notice?"

Mrs. Pinkerton had noticed, from her expression.

"Karen calls it a honk. He doesn't do it too much, though. It's his laugh. And he doesn't laugh a lot at school. Especially today!"

"Why today?"

"Well, we're having this Valentine's Day box and a dance, too, next week, and Walter's all unraveled about maybe not getting any valentines and everyone ignoring him . . ."

"Well, you'll send him one, won't you?" Mrs. Pinkerton asked.

"Oh, sure . . ."

"Well, then he'll get at least one, won't he? And speaking of valentines, I think that's the project Jackie Sue would like you to help her with."

Jackie Sue Pinkerton was nine and in the third grade at the Barker Goodhue Elementary School. Lots of times she could be a pain, but mostly Amanda liked her little sister very much. She was smart like Walter. She could do all her math and she even paid attention to some of the news, but she was very outgoing and friendly and everyone in her class liked her. She always got invited to all the birthday parties in the neighborhood.

"I have too many valentines to send," she explained to Amanda as they sat together on Jackie Sue's bed.

"You have too many?"

"I have to send one to each of my camp

friends, that's about a hundred right there, counting my counselors from last summer and the summer before, and I have to send one to each kid in my class and the kids in the other two third grades, too."

"Jackie Sue, I don't think you *have* to send a valentine to all those kids—"

"No, I *do,* Amanda, really. Because all the third grades are having a valentine box and everyone will expect to get a valentine from me."

"But you're not supposed to sign your name to a valentine. So how will anyone know who sent what, anyway?"

Jackie Sue nodded wisely. "Trust me," she said. "We'll all know."

"We're having a valentine box, too," Amanda said.

"But you're in fifth grade! They don't usually have them after third."

"I know. It was Melissa Goobitz's idea."

"Oh. The one who gets everything she wants."

"Right. We're having a dance, too."

"We're not having a dance," Jackie Sue said. "Thank heaven. But we are having this valentine box. So will you walk me down to Kratchett's so I can buy a whole bunch of those books with the valentines you can punch out? They're not as fancy as the ones with the lace and stuff, but they're all I can afford. And I need hundreds, believe me."

Amanda believed her. She herself would probably only need about eight, counting her parents and Jackie Sue.

"Okay," she said. "But let's go now, because I want to get my homework done before dinner—"

"So you can be free to talk on the phone to Karen and Jen," Jackie Sue finished.

"Let's go, smart mouth," Amanda said.

Kratchett's was the local five-and-ten. They sold everything from sewing equipment to disposable diapers. There was a whole section devoted to greeting cards, and as usual, this time of year, an entire row of valentine cards. Jackie Sue breezed up and down the row in four seconds.

"There's nothing here I want," she announced.

"But you didn't even look at them," Amanda protested.

Jackie Sue shook her head. "Don't need to. I told you, Amanda, it's the books I want. They look like coloring books, you know—big, with paper covers. Probably they'll be mostly red. Come on, help me look."

They walked up and down the aisle, looking and frowning. Finally, Amanda stopped a saleswoman in a pink tunic over red pants.

"Excuse me," she said, "but we're looking for—"

"Those books that have valentine cards to punch out," Jackie Sue finished.

The woman looked from one sister to the other.

"You know," Amanda said, her hands shaping rectangles in the air, "they're about this big, they look like coloring books—"

"And they have dotted lines around each valentine so you can punch them out or cut them," Jackie Sue continued. "And they probably have about fifty—never mind, I see them!" She moved down to the end of the aisle.

"Thank you very much," Amanda said to the confused saleswoman, who watched them go with a blank expression.

"Yeah, see?" Jackie Sue said, picking up a large paper-covered book decorated with pink and red hearts. "This is what I want. I guess I'll need about four books. That should do it."

Amanda flipped through the book. The valentines were silly, most of them cartoons with dumb sayings, but they were fine for kids who didn't want valentines with mushy stuff in them, anyway. They were also inexpensive, just as Jackie Sue had said.

Amanda chewed her lip. These valentine books, she thought . . . lots of valentines . . . *Melissa Goobitz*! What a neat idea . . . and I think it would work perfectly! She smiled to herself.

"Okay," she told Jackie Sue, "let's check these books out and get home."

"But wait, Amanda—I only need four. You've got *five* there."

"I know," Amanda answered. "I just had this incredible brainstorm!"

That night Amanda did manage to get her homework done before dinner, but she didn't spend the rest of the evening on the phone with her friends. She slipped quietly into her room and closed the door. She picked up the extra valentine book she'd bought and flopped down on the floor with it. Then one by one, she punched out each valentine until a pile of them lay in front of her on the rug.

She got up and went over to her desk, where a big mug with the crest of Syracuse University—her dad's alma mater—sat, holding pens and pencils of every color. Amanda brought the mug down to the floor, dumped out all the pens and pencils, and began to write on the valentines. She didn't stop writing until each silly card contained a message, each message in a different color and each in a different handwriting.

All the time she worked, Amanda smiled to herself. She knew it was only Thursday and she had until Tuesday. She had all weekend to do this, if she really stopped to think about it, but she was so excited about her idea that she just couldn't wait, so she worked and worked until her hand hurt.

"He's going to *flip*!" she squealed out loud. "He will absolutely *flip*!"

She was finished at around nine-thirty.

"Amanda!" her mother called from downstairs. "How about some sleep? It's a school night!"

"I know," Amanda called back. "Soon." She picked up some of the cards scattered around her on the rug and continued to smile as she read them to herself. On a drawing of a bodybuilder: "Hi, gorgeous! Be my valentine!" Signed, "Guess Who?" On a cartoon snail: "Don't be slow to call! You're my valentine!" Signed, "The One Who Likes You Best". On a picture of a shooting star: "I'm fallin' for you, valentine." Signed, "A Secret Admirer."

Perfect, Amanda thought. Just perfect.

On Friday, after school, Amanda went to the mall with Karen and Jen and Laura Leff. They read the comic valentine cards on display aloud to each other. They giggled over them and teased each other about the possible recipients, but Amanda didn't say a word about her perfect idea.

Friday night, Mr. Pinkerton brought home Kentucky Fried Chicken and they invited the three Brinkmans over to share it with them. Afterward, they all played Monopoly and Uno and Trivial Pursuit and everyone laughed a lot and had a good time, but Amanda never said a single word about her perfect idea.

On Saturday, the four Pinkertons went to visit Mrs. Pinkerton's mother, called Gram by Amanda and Jackie Sue. Gram baked chocolate chip cookies with the girls while Mr. Pinkerton fixed a broken stair rail and Mrs. Pinkerton looked through the family picture album. They did a lot of talking, but Amanda never said a thing about her perfect idea.

On Sunday, Mr. Pinkerton watched college basketball while Mrs. Pinkerton did the Sunday crossword puzzle. Jackie Sue went across the street to play with a friend and Amanda talked on the phone with Karen. It was a fairly quiet day, but even quieter for Amanda, who never let out a peep about her perfect idea.

On Monday, there was a spelling test

and the class began a new social studies unit on Egypt. Jen was absent with a slight cold, but she promised she'd be back on Tuesday for *sure*. Karen said they'd come drag her out of her house if she didn't show up and Amanda laughed. But she still kept her lips buttoned up about her perfect idea.

Monday night, she could hardly sleep.

She thought about the way she would have to do it.

She couldn't take any chances—no one could catch her. How could she put all those valentines into the box without *somebody* seeing her? Maybe she should ask Melissa how she did it?

4
Broken Heart

The next morning, Amanda was the first one down to breakfast, besides her mother who was always first in the kitchen.

"Well, aren't *you* the early bird," her mother noted.

"I want a ride with Dad today," Amanda said.

"Glad to hear it. Won't the bathroom mirror miss you this morning?"

"Aw, Mom . . ."

"Just teasing, dear. I know every

young girl likes to check herself out a lot. I was a fifth grader myself once, you know."

Amanda looked slyly at her mother. "Uh-huh," she said. "And now that you're somebody's mother, you're much too old to be looking in the mirror, right? Mirrors are only for kids."

Mrs. Pinkerton yanked on one of Amanda's bright curls. "That's right," she said. "Once you get to my age you're just too ancient to think about your looks. Here's some toast. Did you tell Walter to get here early?"

"Uh . . ."

"Well, go call him, Amanda. It's not nice to strand him here. Especially if he's so upset about Valentine's Day, as you explained."

Amanda took a deep breath. She should have thought of this part of it . . . Walter would come to the house and she'd be gone.

"I can't call," she said. "I'll wake up the Brinkmans."

"Amanda, the Brinkmans are up, getting ready for work."

"Oh . . ."

Jackie Sue bounded into the kitchen then.

"Morning," she said. "Can I have grape jelly instead of just butter?" She made a grab for the toast.

"Careful, Jackie Sue, you'll spill—"

"Oh! Ma! I forgot—I need two pink ribbons for my braids today."

"You're not wearing braids," her mother noted.

"I know, but I will be later. It's for a valentine skit we're doing for the other third grades. I'm supposed to be a valentine mailman."

"*Mailman*?" Amanda said, but her mother was out of the kitchen looking for pink ribbons.

"Honestly, Jackie Sue, why you always wait until the last minute to tell me about these things—"

"Ah! Amanda!" Mr. Pinkerton boomed as he came in to the kitchen, smelling of after-shave lotion. "Finally we get to share your company, eh?"

"Yes, Daddy—"

"Good. Well, finish up, now, because I have a breakfast meeting and I have to be on time." He poured himself a cup of coffee and drank it standing up as he thumbed through the morning paper.

"I'm all ready," Amanda said with a grin. Good old Jackie Sue, she thought. Mom forgot all about calling Walter!

"Amanda, wear your scarf!"

"I will, Mom!"

"Now take these, Jackie Sue. They're two different pinks, but I don't think your teacher will mind. Will she be able to braid your hair?"

"I can braid my own hair. Bye, Mom!"

Mr. Pinkerton gave his wife a quick peck on the cheek. "Check the cornflakes box," he said as he grabbed his coat and hat, "for a valentine."

His wife smiled. "You check the glove compartment in your car," she called, and waved to him.

Jackie Sue dashed out the door. Amanda was already in the car.

"Bye!" Mrs. Pinkerton called and waved. "Oh! Amanda—what about—" But the car had already rolled down the drive.

"Walter . . ." she finished lamely.

As she had hoped, Amanda was the first one in the classroom. Even Mrs. Tragg hadn't arrived, or perhaps she had and was still in the teacher's lounge. Amanda didn't know or care—she had the room to herself.

There on Mrs. Tragg's desk was the valentine box. True to Ms. Simms's vision, it was original. There were hearts, but they were royal blue and buff. There was paper lace, but it stuck out of the corners of the box. And the entire creation was covered with shiny Mylar.

Amanda shook her head at it. It didn't matter what it looked like, she thought. It's going to do the trick for Walter Brinkman!

Quickly, she opened her bookbag and took out the huge bunch of valentines she'd stuffed in it. There was a rectangular slit cut into the top of the box and Amanda pushed all of her cards through it. Some got stuck and she had to pull them out and slip them in one by one, but she managed to get all of them into the box before—

"Amanda?"

Amanda jumped.

"I'm sorry, dear, I didn't mean to startle you. You're very early this morning, aren't you?"

It was Mrs. Tragg.

"Yes—uh . . ."

"Did you put your card in?"

"Card?"

"Your valentine card. You did remember to bring one, didn't you?"

Amanda swallowed. She reached into her bookbag and pulled out the cards for her girlfriends and Walter, along with another one. A special one. It had Kenny Eckhart's name on it.

"Good," Mrs. Tragg said. "Just drop them into the box. They'll be the very first ones, I'm sure, since you're the day's first arrival."

Amanda dropped the cards. They fell with a soft *plop*, as they landed on the bunch of cards from the cut-out book.

"I'm glad Melissa had this idea," Mrs. Tragg said. "I know you're all grown up now, but it's fun to hang on to some childhood things once in a while, isn't it?"

Amanda nodded. She agreed that it was.

Walter was the second to arrive that Valentine's Day. He didn't look at Amanda. He didn't look at Mrs. Tragg, either. He kept his head down and dragged his bookbag over to his desk, where he dumped it. He unwrapped his scarf, shook off his coat, and took both over to the closet where he tossed them at a hook and missed. They thudded to the floor and he left them there.

"Hi, Walter," Amanda called.

He didn't answer.

"I'm really sorry about this morning. I wanted to call you, but my dad was in such a hurry to get to work there wasn't time. Anyway, I figured it wouldn't be too bad, since my house was on the way. . . . I mean, you wouldn't lose any time, right?"

Walter sighed heavily and sank down into his seat.

"Come on, Walter, you look like it's the end of the world!"

"Walter? Did you bring a valentine for the box?" Mrs. Tragg asked him.

He looked up for the first time. "Oh," he said. "Yeah." He got up and walked to the front, carrying a mangled white envelope.

It has to be for me, Amanda thought. It's all crumpled and sad, just like Walter.

"Walter, come on! Can't you cheer up a little? Remember what my dad always says?"

" 'Ninety-nine percent of the things you worry about never, never happen,' " Walter intoned.

"That's right, but you should say it as if you mean it. It's true." She got up and walked over to Walter's desk in the back while Mrs. Tragg put some English sentences to correct on the board.

"You know, Walter . . . you always look like you're expecting the world to come to an end every minute," Amanda said.

Walter just sat. If anything, his head seemed to sink lower onto his desk.

"I mean, maybe if you smiled a little bit or said hello to someone every morning, it might make a difference in the way people treat you."

Walter let out a heavy sigh.

"That kind of noise doesn't exactly make people want to jump up and down with excitement at seeing you, Walter," Amanda said.

Finally, Walter looked up at her. His eyes looked watery.

"I'm just not the kind of person that attracts others, Amanda," he said. "It's hard to look happy when you're feeling bad."

"Walter—"

"No." He held up his hand. "It's true. I have a good brain, so there's a better-than-even chance I'll succeed in my chosen career, and perhaps if I'm lucky there will be a nice woman who might marry me someday, though I'm not counting on it—"

"Walter—"

"But I've resigned myself to the fact that I'm doomed to live out my lower-school days as the butt of school jokes." He nodded for emphasis, licked his dry lips, and folded his hands on his desk.

Amanda plunked herself down on the seat in front of him and turned to face him.

"You sound as if you've given this a lot of thought, Walter," she said.

"Oh, I have, Amanda. I have. You're the only friend I have and I know it's only because our parents are so close and we've grown up together. I know you're just being nice."

"Listen, Walter, I'm not being nice!" Amanda was beginning to get angry. "What's got into you all of a sudden, anyway? I don't remember your talking like this before. Is it Valentine's Day? Is that it?"

"It seems to have brought things to a head." Walter sighed again. "Valentine's Day is really just a public popularity contest. It's bad enough to know you're unpopular and now everyone has to see it, too. Do you know what I almost did?"

"What?"

"I almost bought a bunch of cards and wrote my name on them, just to put in the box, so it would look as if I actually got something."

Amanda chomped down on her lower lip.

"But I decided I just couldn't sink that low. So I didn't do it."

Amanda let out her breath.

"But I guess maybe you sent me a card, so at least I won't be the only kid in the class who has absolutely *nothing* to open." He gave her a weak smile. "Thanks in advance, Amanda."

"You're welcome." Amanda stood. She glanced toward the box. Did it look bigger, now that it was stuffed with all her cards? For the first time, she had a few misgivings. Did she do the right thing?

Well, it sure was too late now. . . .

There were Kenny and Mark and Laura and Karen coming through the door right now. Mrs. Tragg had finished the sentences for English and had turned to greet the new arrivals.

Whatever happened now . . . would happen.

5
Love at First Sight

The day seemed to drag for Amanda. Jen had returned to school, even though she sniffled occasionally into a wad of Kleenex.

After they'd finished eating in the lunchroom, the three friends stood together in the hall before going back into their classroom.

"By Bom did't wad me to cub back this sood," Jen told Amanda and Karen, "bud I could't biss Valetide's Day."

"Can you translate that?" Karen asked.

"Her mom didn't want her to come back this soon, but she couldn't miss Valentine's Day," Amanda repeated. "But what about giving us all your cold?"

"Well, which do you care about? Gettig a cold or havig *be* here?"

"Oh, having *you* here, of course." Karen giggled. "What's a bad cold, anyway, between friends? Just stand over there, please, Jen, and breathe in *that* direction."

"Hey—" Amanda began. She was just on the verge of telling them. She was standing on the edge of that cliff, just waiting to drop it all. She needed to know! Was it a good thing she had done? Could it be a harmful thing? It seemed like such a *perfect idea* all weekend long! Even yesterday . . .

"Amanda?"

"Hmm?"

"You look like you're on another planet or something."

"Hmm," Amanda said.

"What is it, anyway? Are you worried about that valentine you sent to Kenny Eckhart?" Karen teased.

"No, I'm not worried—hey! Who told you I sent a valentine to Kenny Eckhart?"

Karen and Jen giggled. "Just a guess," Karen answered.

"Well, how about you?" Amanda pointed to Jen. "Mark Smith!" she said.

Jen nodded and sniffed again. "I'b goig back to the scede of the cribe," she told them. "Bight as well be hubiliated agaid."

"And you, Karen?" Amanda pointed her finger at her friend. "I'll bet it's . . . Andy Moore!"

"Wrong," Karen said, but her cheeks reddened.

"Andy Moore!" Amanda repeated, delighted with herself.

"As a matter of fact, I sent valentines to you and Jen. And now I'm sorry I sent one to *you*."

"Too late," Amanda reminded her, and then thought again of Walter.

"Amanda, you've got that look again," Karen said. "What is it, anyway?"

Amanda inhaled. "Well," she said, "I think maybe I'd better ask you about something. I was going to keep it a secret, but now I'm not so—"

The bell rang.

Fifth graders appeared from nowhere, hurrying to get in the door so as not to be marked late. Someone brushed against Karen, saying a quick, " 'Scuse me!"

"We have to go in," Amanda said.

"Rats! You won't forget to tell us later, will you?" Karen asked.

Once again, Melissa Goobitz stood at the front of the room, eyeing her fellow classmates. "Mmm . . ." she said, peering at each face.

"Oh, come on, Melissa," someone called out. "Just pick anyone!"

"I won't pick just 'anyone,' " Melissa

said. "I'm going to pick just the *right* person."

"Melissa, all we need is someone to hand out the valentines," Laura said.

"Don't make such a big deal out of it," Kenny Eckhart said.

"I pick"— Melissa waved her pointed finger around the room—"Wal-ter Brink-man!"

Amanda's jaw dropped. You're a stinker, Melissa, she thought, but she didn't say it. She turned to see Walter, who had tried to hide himself under his desk and was now appearing to gasp for air in the back of the room.

"Come on, Walter," Melissa said. "We hardly ever hear a peep out of you. It's time you got picked for something. You'll be our valentine mailman!"

Amanda thought about Jackie Sue, the third grade's valentine mailman. At least Walter didn't have to braid his hair.

"Uh, Melissa, I . . ." Walter was choking, but Melissa had already scooted down the aisle to the back and had grabbed him by the hand.

"Up, up, Walter! Let's go!" she was saying. "The whole class is waiting to find out whose valentine is who!"

Amanda was slightly relieved to see that Walter seemed to be bearing up. His face wasn't as red as she'd expected it to be and it wasn't green, either. He wasn't hyperventilating and it looked as though he was pretty steady on his feet. She tried to give him an encouraging smile, but he wouldn't look in her direction. He wasn't looking in any direction.

"Okay, Walter, we're ready," Melissa said.

Walter just stood.

"Okay, Walter. Open the box and take out the valentines!"

Mrs. Tragg moved toward her desk. "Here, let's see if I can be of some help. . . ." She picked up the box and shook it. Then she turned it upside down and shook it some more. "There," she said, "that should mix everything up nicely. Now, let's get the top of the box open with these scissors," she said, and proceeded to cut the Mylar-covered cardboard back from where the original slit was. "There, now, Walter," she said, standing back. "It's all yours."

Walter just stood.

"I'll help!" Amanda said, and stood up.

"No!" Melissa cried. "I picked Walter and it's his honor and he's going to do it by himself."

Mean little witch, Amanda thought and sat down again.

With the whole class staring, Walter finally moved into action. He dumped his hand in the box as if it weren't attached to him and pulled out a handful of cards.

"Call out the name on the envelope, Walter!" Melissa said impatiently. "You know what to do!"

Without looking up, Walter mumbled, "Laura Leff."

"Laura!" Melissa announced. "Pass it back. Next!"

"Kenny Eckhart," Walter whispered.

"Kenny!" Melissa yelled.

Amanda's heart lurched.

"Next! Come on, Walter, we'll be here all day!"

"Oh, give it a rest, Melissa," Karen said, and Mrs. Tragg said, "Girls . . ."

Walter picked up another card. "Uh," he said.

"*What?*" said Melissa.

"Uh . . . it's for me," Walter said.

"For *you?*"

"Yes, Melissa, it's for *him,*" Amanda said clearly. It *had* been a perfect idea after all!

Walter was holding another card. "This one's for me, too," he said, this time above a whisper, but barely.

"Did he say it was for him, too?" Melissa asked.

"Yes, he *did,*" Amanda said.

Walter stood a little straighter. "Mark

Smith," he said. And this time, Melissa didn't have to echo him.

"Karen Stern," Walter said. "And, uh—another one for me."

"*Another* one?" Melissa said. Her eyes were wide.

"Yes, he said another one," Amanda said through tight lips. "Are you having trouble hearing him, Melissa?"

"And"— Walter cleared his throat— "another one for me. . . ." As he stuffed each valentine into his pocket, his voice seemed to get stronger and his back straighter. "And *another* one. And—" A smile was beginning to form on his face. Amanda thought he actually looked— well, *good.* "Hey. Another one for me. . . ."

Amanda beamed.

The class was watching Walter closely now. He seemed to be changing before their eyes. In between a valentine for Laura, Mark, Kenny, Karen, Jen, Amanda, Melissa, and everyone else, there were two, three, four valentines for Walter.

"There have to be at least *twenty*!" Melissa snorted.

Fifty, Amanda thought.

"I bet he put them in himself!" Melissa burst out.

Everyone glared at her.

"You should know," Karen hissed. "Where did your five come from?"

"That was a terrible thing to say, Melissa," Mrs. Tragg said from behind her desk. "Really! I think you owe Walter an apology."

Melissa made a pouty face.

"Hey, if he stuffed that box, he sure is a good actor about it," Mark Smith said. "I sure liked watching him look so surprised. Nice going, Walt!"

"Yeah, nice going!" Kenny Eckhart began to applaud. "Looks like you have a lot of secret admirers in the class, huh? What've you got that I don't?"

And then it happened. Right in front of the whole class.

"Ohhnk! Ohhnk!"

Amanda held her breath. Her eyes widened as she stared at Walter, who had clapped his hand over his mouth.

The class burst into sudden laughter, but it was a very different kind of laughter than either Amanda or Walter had heard before.

And then they were all applauding, as Walter, shifting from one foot to another, was now blushing furiously. But the grin on his face had spread from ear to ear.

"You didn't tell me you were sending a valentine to Walter," Laura whispered to Karen.

"You didn't tell me *you* were," Karen whispered back.

Laura dropped her eyes. Every girl in the whole fifth grade sent Walter Brinkman a valentine and I didn't even know about it, she thought.

Jen blew her nose and looked up at Walter, beaming at the class. He is kind of cute, standing up there like that with that nice smile, she thought. Everyone must have seen it but me. Look at all those cards he got!

Karen was watching Walter, too. You can tell he's no Melissa, she was thinking. *He* didn't write those cards to himself. Mark's right, you can see it on his face. He was just shocked that he got all those cards. He's got that nice shy quality you don't see in boys anymore. Isn't it funny, everyone saw it but me! Amanda was right about Walter all along.

Amanda covered her mouth with her fingers. She was afraid she'd burst into delighted laughter if anyone even glanced at her.

But there was no need to worry. Everyone was looking at Walter. And look at Walter! Amanda couldn't believe it. She'd never seen Walter looking so . . .

So what?

Handsome?

Well, maybe that was too strong a

word. But he sure looked a lot less like a cocker spaniel than he did before.

I shouldn't have been so afraid, Amanda thought. I was right. It was not only a perfect idea, it was an *absolutely* perfect idea!

6

Dreamboat

Mrs. Pinkerton stopped cutting out Abraham Lincoln silhouettes for her next morning's nursery school class and put down her paper and scissors.

"You did what?" she said.

"I wrote out a whole bunch of valentines and put Walter's name on them," Amanda said again.

"Oh, Amanda, that was such a sweet thing to do!"

"I got the idea from Jackie Sue. She probably got at least fifty, and I thought about what Walter's face would look like when he saw he wasn't the most unpopular kid that was ever born."

"Well, what was it like?"

"Mom, it was wonderful! I mean, you could watch him just change his whole personality, right before your eyes! His shoulders went back, his head was up, he was *smiling*. . . ."

"Mmm—Walter Brinkman *smiling*? Well! That must have been worth seeing!"

"It was, Mom. Everyone applauded him. And this is really going to sound weird, but—I swear, he almost looked *taller.*"

Mrs. Pinkerton smiled. "No," she said, "it doesn't sound weird. When you're feeling pretty good about yourself, you look better."

"Really?"

"Really. So what happened after that?"

Amanda took a bite of a cookie and a sip of milk. "Well, after that, we had pizza that Mrs. Tragg sent out for and some punch and stuff. . . ."

"No, I mean what happened with Walter?"

Amanda grinned. "All the girls kept coming up to him, offering him extra pizza and talking to him. I mean, I couldn't believe it. It was neat!"

"Did he say anything to you?" Mrs. Pinkerton asked.

"To me? No. Anyway, I couldn't get near him. He had this big crowd around him. Laura Leff actually asked Walter to save her a dance at the party on Friday."

"Well, Amanda! And no one has any idea you made all the valentines?"

"No! Would you believe I nearly told Karen and Jen? I wasn't sure if I'd done the right thing, and I nearly asked them about it. I would have, too, except everyone started coming back from lunch and there wasn't time. So no one knows. Just you."

Mrs. Pinkerton leaned back in her

chair. "Well, I'd say that was quite an accomplishment, giving Walter that ego boost he needed. But I guess you'll never get a 'thank you' for it."

"Oh, no! That was the idea. Anyway, maybe Walter won't drag himself around so much anymore."

"Amanda, I think you're probably going to be a press agent for a big star someday."

Amanda giggled. "Yeah, maybe a rock group or something."

"Well, what about you? Did *you* get any valentines?"

"Oh. Yeah, I got four. One from Walter and the others are from Karen and Jen and probably Laura."

"Probably?" Mrs. Pinkerton raised her eyebrows.

Amanda sighed. "Yeah, you know. You always send them to your friends. I did last year, even though we didn't have a valentine box."

"Well, the ones your dad and I found in

our room from you were very nice, too. You'll find yours from us on your bed."

"Thanks, Mom."

That night after dinner, the telephone rang. As usual.

"It's for you, Amanda!" Jackie Sue called. "It's Karen—as usual!"

"Thank you," Amanda said. "As usual."

"I don't know why I bother to answer the phone." Jackie Sue sighed.

"Me neither. Hello?"

"Hi, Amanda. Thanks for the valentine."

"Thanks for yours."

There was a pause. "Did you get any others?"

"Uh-huh."

"I mean *besides* from Jen. You probably got one from Walter, huh?"

"Mmm-hmm. I recognize his handwriting."

"Well, you're lucky. I think you're the only girl in our class who got one from him."

"I'm *lucky*?"

"Well, sure! I mean, we've been misjudging him all this time. His smile was so cute, wasn't it? While he was stuffing all those cards in his pocket?"

Amanda smiled at the phone.

"Listen, you have to promise me something," Karen went on.

"What?"

"You have to promise that you'll never tell Walter I didn't send him a card."

Amanda didn't answer.

"Because obviously, I was the only one in the entire fifth grade who didn't. I didn't even tell Jen I didn't send him one. Why do you think she never told us *she* was sending him one?"

"Uh . . ."

"I mean, she is our best friend, isn't she? Do you think all the girls got together and talked about him and then decided to each send him a valentine? Or do you think they all saw what I must have missed all along?"

"Well—"

"Because, Amanda, you were right about him and I was just too dumb to see it. He's got nice shoulders . . . and the way his hair falls, you know kind of behind his ears like that?"

"Gee, Karen, I—"

"And the *wildest* thing of all is that even *Melissa* saw it! Of all people to pick to be the valentine mailman she picked *Walter*! She never picked him for anything before, not even to do the Pledge! But boy, when it came to Valentine's Day, she made exactly the right choice. Boy, have I been *dumb*!"

Melissa picked Walter because she wanted to laugh when he got embarrassed over not getting any valentines, Amanda thought. That's why she picked him! But she didn't say it out loud.

"Anyway, I think Walter's cuter even than Kenny Eckhart. And he likes you, Amanda. He's always liked you."

"Walter and I are friends, like you and I are friends," Amanda said. "He's like my *brother,* Karen!"

"I know, I know," Karen said with a sly note in her voice. "But maybe you should think about him in a different way. I know *I* do."

Amanda decided to change the subject. "Did you get a valentine from Andy Moore?" she asked.

"Oh, Andy Moore!" Karen snorted. "Who cares!"

Amanda rolled her eyes at the ceiling.

The next morning, Walter arrived as usual at Amanda's house and, as usual, she was late.

"Good morning!" he said as she came into the kitchen. He was still wearing his bright smile from the day before. Mrs. Pinkerton was smiling right back at him.

"Doesn't Walter look nice today!" she exclaimed.

He did, actually, Amanda thought. "Uh-huh," she agreed.

"You'll have to hurry with your cereal, Amanda," her mother said. "I don't know why you two don't get a ride with Dad and Jackie Sue."

At least her mother was still the same, Amanda thought.

"I won't be late," she said.

"Amanda was telling me about your newfound popularity, Walter," Mrs. Pinkerton said. "I'm very happy that everyone's beginning to recognize all your wonderful qualities."

"Thanks, Mrs. Pinkerton!" Walter beamed. "And thanks for your valentine, Amanda. Although I'm not really sure which one it was. . . ."

The expensive one, Amanda thought. "You're welcome," she said.

"I'm going shopping this afternoon," Walter said. "My mom's buying me a new pair of slacks. For the dance."

"That's nice," Amanda and her mother both said.

"Yeah . . . you know something, Amanda? Your dad was right. He's a very smart man."

"Right about what?" Mrs. Pinkerton asked.

"His favorite saying: 'Ninety-nine percent of the things you worry about never, never happen.' "

"Oh, that," Mrs. Pinkerton said, and patted Amanda's shoulder. "Yes, he is a very smart man."

Amanda noticed the change as soon as she and Walter got inside the school gates.

"Hi, Walter!" someone called. Walter grinned and waved back.

"Walter, hi!" another voice said. Two voices! Amanda recognized Karen and Jen. What happened to "Hi, Amanda!"?

"Hey, Walt, shoot a couple of hoops before the bell?" Kenny Eckhart called.

"Yeah, *okay*!" Walter called back. "Hey, Amanda, would you carry my bookbag in for me? I'm going to shoot a few with Ken!"

"Right," Amanda said blankly. Shoot a few with Ken! Boy!

She moved to join her friends, who were watching the boys with the basketball.

"Gee, Walter's not bad," Jen said. "Look how he moves. I never saw him play before."

He never did play before, Amanda thought. But he really doesn't look too bad. He passed . . . that was pretty good and that shot . . . wow, it went in! The way he walks . . . it really is different! She put down the two bookbags to watch.

I told him if he smiled and greeted people they'd all treat him differently, Amanda thought. But this is almost a miracle!

"Amanda?" Jen said. "There you are on that other planet again. . . ."

"Oh! No. I was just thinking . . . your cold's all gone, isn't it? I mean, you sound normal again."

"Oh, sure. I'm fine. My mother made me go to bed at eight o'clock, the same time as my little brother, do you believe it? She said if I got enough sleep I'd wake up feeling better. Of course she was right, but I gave her the *hardest* time."

"Another planet," Karen said. "Hey, Amanda, remember yesterday when you were looking off into space and we asked you what was wrong? Remember? You said you wanted to ask our advice about something you did. What was that, anyway?"

"Oh! Oh, that. It wasn't anything. I forgot about it."

Karen frowned. "You sure?"

"Oh, absolutely sure," Amanda said.

That morning, Melissa picked Walter to lead the Pledge of Allegiance. Everyone clapped him on the back as he walked to the front of the room. He grinned at Amanda as he put his hand over his heart.

At the end of lunch, Amanda found

that Walter wasn't sitting at the back of the room anymore. He had moved to the middle of the room and now occupied a desk between Melissa Goobitz and Jen Carter. Amanda waved to him and he waved back.

At the end of gym, a note was sent around to the classrooms that the Girl Scout meeting for that afternoon was canceled. Amanda was glad to have the afternoon free. She thought she might try on some outfits for the valentine dance, or maybe her mother would let her use her lip gloss, or maybe she'd see what the other kids were doing.

At the final bell, Amanda picked up her books and went to get her coat, where she literally bumped into Walter, who seemed to be facing in four different directions at the same time as he chatted with people.

"Sorry," he said.

"It's okay. Are you meeting your mom now?" Amanda asked.

"My mom?"

"Yeah. You know . . . to buy slacks. You said this morning—"

"Oh, right! No, I called her. We're going tonight instead. This afternoon I'm playing some basketball with Ken and the guys. And then I asked them and some of the girls if they wanted to go to the mall."

"You what?"

"Yeah, I thought it would be fun to hang out for a little while. You know, check out the music store and stuff."

Amanda stared at him.

"So, you wanna come?"

"Do I want to come? To the mall with you? And some of the kids?"

Walter tilted his head at her. "That's what I said, didn't I?"

Amanda thought for a moment. "How come you didn't ask me before? If you asked all these kids . . ." She was starting to feel a little hurt.

"Hey, I thought you had Scouts, okay?

Don't have a cow about it, okay?"

Amanda blinked.

"Listen, if you're coming, meet us out at the basketball court. We're not going to be too long. It's pretty cold out."

It's pretty cold in here, too, Amanda thought.

7

A Different Walter

She found Jen heading out the front door of the school.

"Hi," Jen said. "You coming?"

"You mean, Walter's party at the mall?"

"Walter's *party*?"

Amanda shrugged. "That's what it sounds like to me. He 'invited' all his friends to hang out with him at the mall. After he plays basketball, of course."

"Oh, come on, Amanda," Jen said.

Amanda looked at her. "Come on what?" she asked.

Jen looked embarrassed and smiled to cover it. "Oh, you know what I mean," she said.

But Amanda didn't know what she meant and said so.

Jen took a breath, let it out, took another one.

"Well, gee, Amanda . . . I mean . . . you know," she stammered.

But Amanda still glared at her, so she tried again.

"Look," she said, "it took Valentine's Day for everybody to show how they really felt about Walter. I mean . . . we all felt it all along, you know, but no one said anything until we could do it secretly. With anonymous valentine cards."

We? Amanda thought.

"You know how it's easier to do things when you don't have to sign your name. We all liked Walter and well, now he knows it, too. I would think that you, being his real friend, would be happy for him. But you sound . . ."

"What? I sound what?"

Jen made a face. "Funny, that's all."

"Funny?"

"Jealous, okay? Honest, Amanda you sound jealous. Like you still want Walter all to yourself, you know? I mean, I can't say that I really blame you, but—"

"Jen! Give me a break!" Amanda interrupted. "I wasn't talking about *me*. I was talking about *Walter*. I was talking about the way he's changing. I mean, you know how sweet he always was? I mean, yeah, he snorted, but still, he was just . . . *nice*. And now the *nice* part doesn't seem to be there."

Jen shrugged. "He seems the same to me," she said, and Amanda realized Jen really didn't know Walter because she hadn't paid much attention to him before. Except to tease Amanda about him, that is. "So anyway, let's forget it." Jen touched Amanda's arm. "I didn't mean to hurt your feelings, honest, Amanda. You're my best friend. I just didn't want the other kids to hear you say anything bad about Walter. That's all. Because then they'd say—"

"I was jealous."

"Yeah." Jen nodded.

"Well, I'm not."

"Okay. So, are you coming? To the mall?"

Amanda had been about to refuse. She was feeling a little angry with almost everyone about now, but she decided to swallow her pride and go along.

Maybe Jen's right, she thought. I'm not jealous of Walter, but I guess it would look that way.

So she bundled up in her jacket and scarf and followed Jen out of the school toward the basketball court.

The mall wasn't crowded. It was nearly four o'clock on a weekday afternoon, a month and a half past Christmas, and the weather was damp and overcast, so only shoppers who really needed something had dropped by.

There were the usual high school and junior high kids who used the mall as their home away from home, but "Walter's party" seemed to be the only group of elementary school children there without their parents.

"Great!" Walter said. "We have the place almost to ourselves!"

"Yeah! You wanna check out the new releases?" Kenny Eckhart asked, referring to the new tapes at the music store.

"Okay. Or we could play the games out in front of the pharmacy."

"Let's go to Teenswear," Melissa suggested. "The boys can play the electronic games and stuff and we can meet them after. We can get some stuff to eat then."

"I don't want to go to Teenswear," Karen complained. "I don't have any money. It would *kill* me to see something I just love and not be able to get it!"

"You could come back another time and get it," Melissa sniffed.

"Not everyone's parents buy them

everything they want just because they want it," Karen said. But she didn't look at Melissa.

"Well, *I'm* going to Teenswear," Melissa said. "Want to come along, Jen? Amanda?"

"I'll come," Laura said. "I need some stuff for my hair."

"I think I'll watch the games," Amanda said, and some of the others decided they wanted to watch, too.

There were several arcade games lined up outside Reese's Pharmacy and Kenny, Mark, and Walter grabbed the most popular ones first.

"Hey," Jen complained. "Karen said she wanted Pac Man!"

"First come, first served," Walter said with a grin and plunked his quarter in the slot.

He never played those games, Amanda thought, and she didn't know whether to smile or not. He always thought they were silly. He liked some games on the computer, but those were—

Her thoughts were broken by Karen, nudging her. "Isn't he cute?" Karen whispered. "He doesn't really get it. The game, I mean."

She thinks that's cute? Amanda asked herself.

"I could beat him easily!" Karen whispered, and giggled.

"Well, do it," Amanda said.

"No, I'll do better," Karen decided. "I'll teach him."

She stepped up next to Walter and explained the game. She spoke softly, encouragingly, and soon Walter was playing better. He grinned at Karen each time he scored and she grinned back and patted him on the back. When he saw his score printed out on the screen at the end, he burst into an excited honk!

Amanda looked around. No one laughed.

When the game was over, Walter broke away from the group and announced he was heading for the music store.

As he passed Amanda, who had been standing toward the back of the little group, she grabbed his coat sleeve.

"You could have thanked Karen," she told him. "Would have been nice . . ."

Walter made a face at her. "Hey, you think I didn't know how to play that game? I knew."

Amanda clicked her tongue against her teeth.

"Yeah, well, I did."

"Really!" Amanda said in her loudest whisper. "Then what were you doing, giving the poor girl a thrill, letting her help you?"

"Hey, maybe *she* likes to help people," Walter said, and brushed past Amanda.

In the mall, Walter dominated the CD and tape discussion. But Amanda knew he really did know music and had very definite tastes. The group of classmates seemed to hang on his every word and peered at the tiny paragraphs of information on the labels as he spoke.

"So even though his voice isn't that great," Walter was saying, "it really works for rock. I mean, if his voice were better, it wouldn't fit these songs so well. You know, just picture a good, quality sound singing those lyrics in that kind of way he does . . . it'd never work."

"Yeah," Mark agreed, frowning. "I see what you mean."

They were all nodding.

"Yeah, but what about this group?" Jen asked, holding up a small plastic tape box.

"Oh, they're different," Walter said. "Their stuff has important lyrics. They're not just telling a story, they're making a point. You need a believable sound for that, no screaming. The background isn't as loud, either, you notice?"

Amanda watched the others nodding. He does have a lot to offer, she thought, but he always did. No one cared until they thought everyone else cared, too.

The group met Melissa and Laura at the Nathan's Famous Hot Dog stand and they all sat around at one of the tables, laughing and talking about the dance.

"Boys wear suits," Melissa said.

"Yeah, right," Kenny said, and he laughed.

"I mean it. You never wear suits except at weddings and things. It would be nice if you wore suits. We girls are wearing our best stuff, right?" She looked around the table.

"I was going to wear slacks," Karen said.

"No slacks! Not even dressy ones. We're all wearing party dresses and stockings!" Melissa announced.

"I don't mind wearing a sport jacket," Walter said.

"See? Walter is the only one with any taste," Melissa said, and folded her arms.

Mark shrugged. "Sport jackets are okay, I guess. I don't even have a suit."

The others didn't either, but they wouldn't admit it.

"I got a new dress and new shoes," Melissa said smugly.

Karen wrinkled her nose in Melissa's direction. "I'm wearing slacks," she said.

When they'd finished their hot dogs and colas, they each headed off from the mall in different directions, calling good-byes to each other at the door.

Walter and Amanda fell in together naturally, but for a while, neither spoke. Then, Amanda couldn't stand it anymore.

"So," she said. "Feeling better?"

Walter looked blank. "I wasn't sick," he said.

"I don't mean that. I mean about yourself. And your life. A couple of days ago, you couldn't wait for junior high, remember? You said you'd be treated differently in a new environment."

Walter looked at the snow beneath his feet. "I did?" he asked.

Amanda made that clicking noise with her tongue again. "Come *on,* Walter! I was there!"

"I just don't remember, that's all."

"So now, it's all changed, right?" Amanda prodded. "It doesn't matter about junior high anymore because people are treating you differently right now. Right, Walter?"

Walter looked very uncomfortable. "People are okay, Amanda. Just cut it out . . . y'know?" He turned and walked away.

"He won't talk about it," she told her mother. "It's as if . . . things were always this way. Walter was always popular and it never was any different. I can't believe it."

"I can't imagine Walter the way you described," Mrs. Pinkerton said. She kept touching her lips with her fingers. "I mean—Walter?"

Amanda nodded vigorously.

"Well, I mean, you were right. He did stand straighter when I saw him this morning, and of course, there was that *smile*."

"You know what he said when I asked him why he hadn't said anything to me about going to the mall? He said"—she mimicked him—" 'Don't have a cow about it, Amanda!' "

" 'Don't have a cow about it?' "

"Uh-huh."

Mrs. Pinkerton began to laugh.

"It's not funny, Mom."

"No, no, I guess it isn't," Mrs. Pinkerton agreed.

Amanda was on her bed doing her homework when Jackie Sue tiptoed in.

"You busy?" she asked.

"Yes."

"Well, stop being busy. I want to ask you something. It's about Walter Brinkman."

Amanda put down her pencil and turned her head to face Jackie Sue. "What about Walter Brinkman?"

"Well, I didn't mean to overhear, but I happened to be in the tub when you were talking to Mom and I happened to hear you telling about how different Walter is."

Amanda closed her eyes and dropped her head to the pillow. That was all she needed. Miss Congeniality from the lower school knowing about what happened with Walter.

"Jackie Sue, why don't you call one of your friends and have a nice long talk before dinner?" she suggested.

"We don't talk on the phone, remember? You don't start that until fifth grade. Anyway, I really want to know. What happened to Mr. Nobody-Likes-Me?"

"He never said that."

"He did, too. He says it all the time."

Not anymore, Amanda thought. Aloud, she said, "Well, if you have to know . . . he doesn't think that way anymore."

"He doesn't? Why not?"

Amanda decided with an inward sigh that the truth was probably best, but not necessarily the *whole* truth.

"Well, actually, he was worried about Valentine's Day and the dance and everything, but I told him what Daddy always says whenever we're unhappy—"

" 'Ninety-nine percent of the things you worry about—' "

" 'Never, never happen.' And Daddy was right again because Walter got some valentines after all."

"I know," Jackie Sue said softly. "And they were all from you, right?"

Amanda's mouth opened. "How did *you* know?" she asked.

"Well, I may be young, but I'm not dumb. You bought that extra valentine book at Kratchett's and you spent hours and hours in your room with them spread all over the floor and on your bed and everything—"

"My door was closed!" Amanda snapped.

"Not every second, it wasn't. Besides, you had the only green pencil and I came in to borrow it and I just happened to see Walter's name on every single—"

Amanda glowered at her.

"I didn't say anything to anyone," Jackie Sue said, holding up her hands. "I swear!"

Amanda sighed.

"So the valentines made him feel better, but now he thinks he's king-of-the-hill, right? Like you told Mom."

"Well . . ."

Jackie Sue nodded. "I know, I've seen this before."

"Jackie Sue—"

"I *have*. On TV."

"Jackie Sue—"

"A-man-da, I have seen this on the tube!"

"Seen what?"

"It was an old movie. You know, in black and white, no color?"

"*What* was?"

"*Frankenstein,* that's what!"

"*Frankenstein?*"

"Yeah! This guy, he's a doctor or something, and he wants to make a real human being out of old parts or something—"

"I know," Amanda said, sitting up. "I've seen *Frankenstein*. . . . The doctor does this experiment to see if he can make a real person in his laboratory—"

"Right! And he does it! Only the person he makes turns out to be a monster, and it's totally out of this doctor's hands anymore. . . ."

Amanda leaned back against her headboard.

"And in the end, he had to be destroyed," Jackie Sue finished. "It was neat. And that's what I thought of when you said how Walter changed. You made a new person out of him. Don't you think it sounds like the same story?"

"*No,* I don't think it sounds like the same story," Amanda said loudly, and hoped her face hadn't turned red. "Nobody built a new Walter in the laboratory and he's not a monster who has to be destroyed in the end. It was just the opposite. People made him feel wanted so now he feels better and he behaves as though he feels better and that's all. Now go back to your room and let me finish my homework!"

Jackie Sue jumped off the bed. "Okay, okay. I just thought you said you don't like the way Walter has changed and that's what made me think of—"

"Out!"

Jackie Sue got out.

Amanda leaned back on her pillow. It's not the same story, she said to herself. Walter's not a monster. And I'm not the doctor who has to destroy him. She sat up quickly. That's nuts! she thought.

8
Jealousy

The next morning, Amanda came into the kitchen, where her mother asked why she couldn't be earlier so she could get a ride with her father and sister. There was cereal in a bowl with a banana in it and it was still cold outside, but there was one change.

Walter didn't come by to call for Amanda.

At a quarter to nine, he still hadn't arrived. Mrs. Pinkerton was frowning at the clock.

"Do you suppose he's sick?"

"No . . ."

Mrs. Pinkerton picked up a box of colored construction paper she was taking to work and put it on the kitchen table. Then she leaned on the box and looked at Amanda.

"You think this is part of Walter's big change?"

Amanda put down her spoon. "Mom, has Walter ever *ever* missed calling for me?"

"Well . . ."

"I mean, even when we called to tell him I was sick, he *still* 'dropped by' anyway, just in case I got better in the last ten minutes."

Mrs. Pinkerton smiled.

"It's not funny, Mom."

"You're right, it's not."

"I feel like the Walter we knew moved away or something, and this weird clone moved into his house and took over his body."

Mrs. Pinkerton took Amanda's coat off the coatrack and brought it to her. "Sounds like you've been watching too much TV, Amanda."

"Mmm." She thought about Jackie Sue's description of the Frankenstein movie. "Maybe I should've paid better attention," she said.

Walter was playing basketball in the playground when Amanda got to school, so she didn't get to say anything to him until they met at the door to their homeroom when the bell rang.

"Hi," Walter said, and moved toward the closet.

"Wait a minute." Amanda grabbed his sleeve. "Did you notice something different about this morning?"

Walter swallowed. "Uh, different?"

"Walter Brinkman, have you ever missed calling for me on a school day?" Amanda put her hands on her hips and glared at him.

Walter scratched his head. "Oh. Yeah," he said. "Listen, I just left early this morning. I wanted to get here to—you know. . ."

"Shoot some hoops."

"Yeah."

"A call would have been nice."

The corners of Walter's mouth turned down. "Yeah, well, you didn't call me when you came to school early on Tuesday, did you?"

Amanda drew in her breath. "But that was different! That was because—" She stopped. She realized she couldn't really finish. She couldn't tell Walter that she had come to school early with the valentines she'd made for him.

"So now we're even," Walter said. "Besides, I met your dad and Jackie Sue outside and they gave me a ride. You should really get up earlier and go with them," Walter said. "I mean, why throw away a free ride?" He pushed his way into the room.

"Wal-ter!" Melissa squealed. "Listen, I want you to hear this tape I bought yesterday at the mall! It was one you said you liked and maybe we could play it tomorrow at the valentine dance."

"Oh. Sure, Melissa—"

"I brought my Walkman so you could hear it at lunch."

"Great."

"I *know* you'll love it! *Ohhnk*!" Melissa snorted.

Amanda stared at her.

In the lunchroom that day, Amanda watched the group of kids surrounding Walter at his table. There were kids from the other two fifth grades gathered, too, and Walter seemed to be talking to them all about the music that would be played on the stereo at tomorrow's dance. Everyone was smiling. Everyone was nodding. Everyone was making Amanda sick.

"He really knows what he's talking

about, doesn't he?" Karen said. She was sitting next to Amanda picking pieces of green pepper out of her tuna fish sandwich.

"Yeah," Amanda said, "he does. He knows music."

"Funny we never really talked to him much before. I didn't really appreciate him. You did, though. You were right, Amanda."

Amanda didn't say anything. She *had* been right then, she thought, but right now she wasn't feeling so appreciative.

"I told my mother *please* don't put green peppers in my tuna," Karen complained, "and she said, 'Then make your own sandwich,' so of course, I didn't have anything to say to that. . . ."

"Amanda?" Jen said. She, too, was watching Walter and his groupies. "Do you think Walter might ask me to dance tomorrow? I mean, has he ever mentioned me to you?"

Amanda looked at her friend. Her eyes were wide.

"I'm not kidding," Jen said.

"I know," Amanda said. Jackie Sue was right, she thought. I made a monster! Just like Frankenstein.

"So, what do you think?" Jen said.

"As far as I know," Amanda answered, "Walter Brinkman never once danced a single step in his whole life."

"Oh, Amanda, really, you're funny," Jen said.

Amanda had had enough. She sat up straight in her chair and looked at the two girls who had been her best friends since they were all in kindergarten.

"Listen," she said. "Are you the same people who used to kid me about being friends with Walter all these years? Don't you remember? I mean, it was only *Monday* you were teasing me for walking to school with him. Right before he got all those valentines! Remember?"

Karen made a face. "I told you, Amanda, we were wrong. I mean, I apologized and everything. You were right and we were wrong, what more can I say?" She spread her arms wide.

"That's not what I mean!" Amanda was exasperated. "I *mean*—what changed your minds about Walter? What made you think he was the hottest thing on the planet all of a sudden? What *was* it?"

Karen and Jen looked at each other.

"It was the valentines!" Amanda said. *Forget* about keeping it secret! she thought. Now I'm mad! "It was the valentines, remember? You only started to think Walter was so cool after you thought everyone *else* thought so!"

Jen slurped milk through her straw and put down the container. "Amanda, listen, remember what I said to you yesterday?"

"I remember!" Amanda said. "You thought I was jealous, but I'm not! Honest! I'm just mad!"

"Mad? Why?" Karen asked.

"Because Walter was nice before everyone thought he was, and now he *isn't* anymore. Because I wanted Walter to feel more popular so *I* was the one who sent him the valentines and all it did was make him a big conceited *jerk*! And now that he's a big conceited jerk, *you* think he's *terrific*! So that's why I'm *mad*!"

Karen and Jen looked at each other again. Then they looked at Amanda.

"It's true!" Amanda yelled. The lunchroom quieted down and everyone looked at her.

"It's okay," Jen said, smiling. "We just spilled something. It's okay."

The room picked up its noisy hum again.

"Listen, Amanda," Karen said, "we won't say anything to anyone about this, so don't you, either."

"You don't believe me?" Amanda stared at them.

"Oh, come on, Amanda, *you* sent all those valentines? There must have been thirty, or thirty-five—"

"Fifty," Amanda said.

"You sent fifty valentines to Walter

Brinkman," Jen said. She and Karen giggled.

"I did! It took me an entire *night,* practically! My *hand* even hurt!"

The bell rang and Karen and Jen stood up. "Listen, Amanda—we're your best friends and we promise we won't tell anyone, okay? But just admit you feel kind of funny about not having Walter all to yourself anymore and then you'll feel better," Jen said. She and Karen went to dump their trash in the bins near the door.

That night at supper, Amanda told Mr. Pinkerton the whole story and the family spent the meal discussing it.

"*I* think you should tell Walter you sent him those valentines," Jackie Sue said firmly. "Then maybe he'll get down off his throne!"

"Oh, no!" Amanda cried. "I couldn't do that."

"Why not? He's already popular now,

so that part's okay, and if you tell him, then maybe he won't be such a stinker to you."

"It's not about that," Amanda insisted. "He really changed. I mean—I used to like Walter and now I don't. He's a *whole other person*!"

Mr. Pinkerton shook his head. "I don't know, Amanda." He looked at Jackie Sue. "We gave him a lift this morning, remember? He seemed the same to me. How'd he seem to you?"

"Well . . . I asked him if he told Amanda he was riding with us and he said he'd 'catch her at school.' "

Mr. Pinkerton shrugged. "So?"

"So, Daddy, if you really know Walter Brinkman, he's never done anything like that in his life. He *always* goes in and calls for Amanda."

"Even when I'm sick," Amanda said.

"Even when she's sick," Jackie Sue said.

Mr. Pinkerton said, "Hmph."

"Tell him," Jackie Sue said again. "Tell Walter what you did. You don't have to tell anyone else."

But Amanda shook her head unhappily. "I already told Karen and Jen, but they said I was just jealous and they didn't believe me."

"Some friends," Jackie Sue grumbled.

"I guess I can see how they'd feel that way," Amanda said. "I might not believe me either if I weren't me."

"Well, *I'd* believe you," Jackie Sue said loyally.

"So, honey, what are you going to do?" Mrs. Pinkerton asked.

"I just don't know," Amanda said.

That night, Amanda picked out her outfit for the valentine dance. She had a pretty red cotton sweater with a lace collar that she saved for special occasions and a red-and-blue print skirt that went perfectly with it. Red for Valentine's Day. A perfect idea.

She sat on her bed with the outfit in her lap.

Karen will probably wear slacks, she thought. And Melissa will be mad. Good. It's none of Melissa's business what someone wears. Oh, well, maybe Melissa will be too busy trying to get Walter to dance with her to notice what we're all wearing.

No, Amanda smiled to herself, she'll notice!

She picked up her schoolbag and dumped its contents out on her desk. Out fell her four valentines.

"I forgot about these," Amanda said out loud, and picked them up.

"This one's from Karen, I can tell. 'Roses are red, violets are blue. I feel dumb, sending this to you.' " Amanda laughed. Definitely Karen. "And this one's Jen's. 'I'm glad you're my friend, valentine!' " she read. I'm glad, too, she thought. And Walter's. It was a picture of a cute Snoopy dog inside a big red heart.

"Happiness is a warm puppy," it read, "and having you for a friend." Amanda bit her lip.

Then there was the last one.

Yes, it was Laura's handwriting, Amanda was sure. Laura always drew those have-a-nice-day faces on her notes and this one had a big smiley one right on the back. "Could you guess," it read, "that I wanted you for my valentine?" It was red, covered with question marks with that face drawn on the back, and signed in ballpoint, "Your Friend." Typical Laura. Not very original, not really funny, just kind of . . . nice.

With a sigh, Amanda opened her desk drawer and dropped the valentines in with the ones she had received from her family.

I just can't tell Walter, she thought as she leaned back in her chair. Everybody likes him a lot now and I guess he's happy. If I liked him better before, then maybe that's *my* problem, not his.

But I sure will miss my friend. . . .

9
The Dance

Since it would be silly to go home and change after lunch, the fifth grades had voted to wear their party clothes to school in the morning. Melissa had pushed for it.

"It'll be so nice to be dressed up for a change," she'd said. "We never see anybody in anything except jeans and sweatshirts."

Amanda had to admit that for once, Melissa was right. There was Jen in a pink wool suit with a bright red bow in her long blond hair. She got that suit for her cousin's wedding at Christmastime, and she really looked pretty in it.

And Karen *did* wear slacks, but they were dressy: powder blue with a soft white sweater and her big sister's gold locket on a chain.

Were they wearing lip gloss? Amanda hoped so. *She* was!

And Walter. He hadn't picked her up again that morning, but she hadn't really expected him. Now, there he was, trying so hard to look cool, leaning against Mrs. Tragg's desk, talking to Mark Smith.

Amanda looked harder. Yes, he must have gotten new slacks, she thought. She didn't remember seeing that pair on him before. A soft gray, topped by a blue blazer. He did look fine, she had to admit. She waved to him and pointed to his outfit as she pantomimed applause, but all he did was raise his chin at her.

She turned to hang up her jacket and

bumped into something yellow.

It turned out to be a V-necked sweater on Kenny Eckhart.

" 'Scuse me," Amanda said, and blushed.

"It's okay."

"Nice sweater," Amanda said.

"Uh . . ." He nodded, blushed. "Yeah. Nice, uh . . ." He gestured at her outfit and she nodded and blushed. Then he was gone, moving toward the front of the room and Walter Brinkman.

"Hey, we look great," Karen said as she spotted Amanda. "I'm the only one in slacks."

"But you're still dressed up," Amanda told her.

"Tell Melissa," Karen snapped. "She practically told me to go home and change!"

Amanda laughed. "And what did you 'practically' tell *her*?"

"Nothing. I felt too good. Guess what they're serving this afternoon? I found out from Mrs. Gantz in the principal's office."

"Pizza. That's what they always serve."

"Not today. They're serving a pink-and-red heart-shaped cake and pink punch."

"Ick, I think I'd rather have pizza," Amanda said.

"Well, me, too, but that's not all. We're also having pink and red cookies, personally baked by Mrs. Goobitz."

"Melissa's *mother*?"

"The same."

"But she baked the cookies for the third-grade picnic and all the kids—"

"Euked, I know. But she used green coloring on them. These are pink. Maybe there's a difference."

"Are you going to find out?"

"Me? Are you crazy?"

"I think we should send out for pizza," Amanda said.

"Well . . ." After a moment, Karen said, "Who'll you dance with?"

"Today?"

"No, three years from now at eighth-grade graduation. Of *course* today!"

Amanda caught her lower lip between her teeth and looked around the room. "I don't know," she said. "Whoever asks me. If someone does . . ."

"Hey, *you* can ask someone, too, you know. You have a mouth."

Amanda blushed. "I guess. . . ."

"*I'm* asking Walter."

"Well, he'll like that," Amanda said.

"You think?"

"Uh-huh."

"Are you asking—" Karen began, but Mrs. Tragg had taken her place at the head of the class and everyone had begun to sit down.

"Well!" Mrs. Tragg clapped her hands together and held them in front of her. "I started to address you as usual as 'boys and girls,' but looking at you here, dressed so nicely and looking so grown up, I feel I must call you all 'ladies and gentlemen.' "

Several of the boys snickered.

"I hope," Mrs. Tragg continued, "that you conduct yourselves as ladies and gentlemen today and I hope you all enjoy the dance later this afternoon. Now, Melissa, will you start us off with the Pledge, please?"

Andrea Borden was the only child in Mrs. Tragg's room who hadn't worn something special for today. She had on a skirt and top that were perfectly presentable, but they were similar to the clothes the girls wore every day. Either she had forgotten about the dance or she didn't have any dress-up clothes, but she sat scrunched up in her seat as if she were embarrassed about what she did have on.

Melissa picked Andrea to lead the Pledge.

Amanda ground her teeth together.

Most of the class tried hard to pay attention, but it was hard. It was Friday, for one thing, and for another, they would be dismissed early for the dance. Besides, every time they turned around, they saw their own classmates looking quite different and special. Everyone was in a festive mood.

When the science tests were passed back, Mrs. Tragg complimented Laura Leff on getting the highest grade. It was the first time in Amanda's memory that Walter had not received the highest grade in science. She glanced over at him, but he was joking with Mark Smith and wasn't even paying attention.

The day managed to drag on. Everyone seemed to be squirming in his or her seat. Amanda was beginning to wish that Valentine's Day had never been an actual holiday on the calendar when Mrs. Tragg finally told them they could put away their books and form a line. It was time to go to the gym.

The gym did look beautiful. The lights had been dimmed and all the decorations they had made looked pretty and festive as they hung from the ceiling and from all the ropes and cables above. There were huge red hearts (red, in spite of Ms. Simms) trimmed in white lacy paper that were hung from the basketball backboards and on the walls.

A long table with a satiny pink tablecloth had been set up at one end of the gym, manned by teachers and Melissa Goobitz's mother, ready to serve the refreshments.

There were two large stereo speakers mounted at each end of a long platform and music was already playing: a soft rock song that was intended to put everyone in the mood for dancing.

They filed in awkwardly.

Now that the time had finally arrived, everyone seemed a little nervous.

"Do you feel stupid?" Jen whispered to Amanda. "I do. I mean, I really feel stupid."

"Why?"

Jen shrugged. "I don't know. What do we do, stand around in a line, like we're all on sale at Kratchett's or something?"

Amanda giggled. "No, we can do whatever we want. We can eat, we can sit, we can talk. We can ask someone to dance."

"*Would* you?" Jen asked.

"Would she what?" Karen wanted to know.

"Ask someone to dance."

"Of course she would! I'm going to! I'm asking Walter Brinkman. And you should ask Mark if he doesn't ask you."

Jen grinned. "Maybe I'll ask Andy Moore," she said.

"I don't like Andy Moore anymore," Karen sniffed.

Laura appeared next to them with a paper cup of pink punch. "It's a little sweet," she told them, "but it's not bad. Look who's dancing . . ." She pointed toward the middle of the gym floor.

"Melissa?" Karen said. "Who's that she's with?"

They all craned their necks. "It's that kid from Mr. Harris's room, the one who plays the clarinet," Amanda said.

"Oh, yeah . . . the one in the Christmas pageant who went flooey and nearly pierced all our eardrums with that squeaky note." Jen clapped her hands over her ears and drew in her breath. "When I think about it, I can still hear it!"

"I'm getting something to eat," Karen said, and began to head toward the refreshment table.

"Me, too—wait!" Jen hurried after her.

Laura sipped from her cup. "Looks pretty, huh?" she said.

"Mmm," Amanda agreed.

"Dances are fun, but I still think girls like them better than boys," Laura said.

Amanda was beginning to wonder how much she herself liked dances.

"I bet I can dance better than any boy in this room," Laura said. "And I bet you can, too."

Maybe, Amanda thought, but that wasn't the point. . . . "It might not matter how well you can dance if no one wants to dance with you," she told Laura.

They looked around the room. The girls seemed to be lumped in one corner of the room and the boys were crowding the refreshment table. Melissa was dancing and so were a few other boys and girls, but most of the crowd was just—

"Hey, look!" Laura was pointing.

Amanda looked.

Karen and Walter were in the middle of the room. They were bobbing and shaking and twirling as the music played louder. Several people had stopped dancing and talking to watch them.

"He's not too bad. . . ." Amanda observed.

"He can't dance at all," Laura said, and giggled, "but he's trying so hard, he actually looks cute! Look at him bounce!"

"And Karen can do it, of course."

"But they're having so much fun,

aren't they? Oh, Amanda, I think I want to dance, too. Come on." Laura began to move toward the groups, which seemed to be coming together in the center of the floor.

Soon, almost everyone was dancing. No one really needed a partner, either. Boys and girls just jumped in and began to move to the music as best they could, sometimes facing someone, sometimes not.

Now the ice was broken. Teachers breathed sighs of relief. The classes were having a good time.

10
From Your Valentine

The sky had begun to darken outside. The dance would be over before too long. Amanda had just finished her cake and punch and was about to get up to dance again, when she saw Walter coming toward her.

So, he's going to ask me to dance, she thought. It sure is about time. Except I don't even know if I want to dance with him now. He's asked just about everyone here except me. . . .

She looked at Walter's determined

face and she almost laughed. Wow, she thought. A few days ago, I wouldn't have even wanted Walter to ask me to dance. The kids would have teased me. And I would have been waiting for Kenny. She blushed. Or someone.

It's true. Walter would have been a pain, asking me to dance and honking at me, even though he was nice to walk to school with and talk to. . . .

Hmm. Amanda frowned at these new thoughts. And here came Walter. She noticed he had pulled his shoulders back and sucked in his stomach.

Amanda shook her head. And now he's a big shot and I'm glad he finally came over to me. Guess that doesn't make *me* very nice, does it?

"Hi, Walter." She waggled her fingers at him.

"Hya. *Onnnk, onnnk*!"

Amanda sighed. "I can see you're really having a good time, huh?"

"Oh. Yeah. Listen, Amanda, can I ask you something?"

"What?" Here it comes, Amanda thought, and held out her arms for the dance.

"Do you know Daphne French?"

"Huh?" Amanda dropped her arms.

"Daphne French. She's in Mr. Harris's class. See? She's over there. The girl with the black hair, wearing the blue thing."

Amanda stared at the spot where Walter was pointing.

"Yeah," she said, "I've seen her around."

"But do you *know* her?"

"No, not really. Do you want to dance or not?" Amanda was losing patience.

"Yeah! I do! But I felt kind of funny just going up to someone I don't know and asking her to dance!"

Amanda rolled her eyes to the ceiling, but Walter didn't notice.

"So anyway, I thought if you knew her, maybe you could introduce us. But you don't, right? So forget it." He turned away.

Amanda put her hands on her hips.

"Walter!" she called after him.

His head swung around. "Yeah?"

But she didn't say anything. She just stood there until he wrinkled his nose at her and moved off.

"Amanda, isn't this the best dance?" Karen had appeared at her side. "I danced with Walter twice! The first time I asked him, but the second time he asked me. He's not too good, but he sure has energy, doesn't he? I think we got everyone else in the spirit, too, don't you? Honestly, that Walter . . ."

"Uh—I'm going to the girls' room," Amanda said, and she hurried out one of the back doors into the hall.

Once alone, she leaned up against the cool, ivory-colored wall.

That Walter, she thought, Karen's phrase echoing in her mind. I wanted him to feel better about himself and now he does, so should I be mad because he's not the same person he was before? Because he doesn't need me to whine to anymore? I should be *glad* he doesn't need me to whine to anymore!

She curled a lock of hair with her finger and smoothed her dress. She shook her shoulders and took a deep breath. Then she turned and walked back into the gym.

She had just reached the dance floor when she felt a tap on her shoulder and heard a coarse whisper in her ear.

"Amanda!"

"Walter?"

"Somebody's looking for you."

"Who?" Amanda turned to face him. He had a big grin on his face.

"Never mind," Walter said. "I didn't see you for a few minutes, but now that you're here, I'll tell the person where to look."

"Walter, what . . ."

But all she got from Walter was an *"Onnnk!"* before he hurried away.

That Walter, she sighed again, and craned her neck to see what he was up to. There he was—talking to someone in a yellow sweater. . . .

And now that someone was coming over. To her!

They stood together at the back of the gym. Their faces were flushed from dancing and they were holding cups of punch. Amanda was about to bite into a pink cookie.

"You sure you want to do that?" Kenny Eckhart asked. "That's a Goobitz cookie, you know."

Amanda grinned. "I know. But we tested them out on Melissa first. She ate a whole plateful of them before and she's still dancing, so I guess they must be okay."

"Hey, Amanda?"

"What?"

"Nothing."

Amanda finished the cookie and looked at him. "What?" she asked again.

Kenny was examining his fingernails.

"You get a lot of valentine cards?" he asked.

Amanda shrugged. "Not a lot."

"You remember one with a happy face on it?"

"Oh, the one from . . ." Laura?

"From me," Kenny said.

Amanda looked at him. He was still studying his nails.

The fourth valentine hadn't been from Laura. The not too funny, not too original, but nice valentine had been from Kenny Eckhart.

"Kenny?"

"Yeah?"

"Did you get a Dick Tracy valentine?"

Now he looked at her. "From *you*?" he asked.

She nodded.

"Hey," he said.

"Last dance, ladies and gentlemen," one of the teachers was announcing into the microphone. "This is the last dance. Please be careful going home. There are some parents outside waiting, so make sure yours aren't here before you start walking. Thank you all for your cooperation and we hope you've had a good time this afternoon."

There was a smattering of applause from the floor.

"Hey, Amanda!"

She turned. It was Walter and he was grinning widely. Walter Brinkman, not just smiling but actually grinning! Who would have believed it!

"Listen, I've decided to give you the thrill of having the last dance with guess who—me! So!" Walter made a fancy bow.

Kenny began to laugh and slapped Walter on the shoulder. "Hey, Walt!" he said.

"Sorry," Amanda said, "but I'm dancing the last dance with Kenny, Walter."

"Oh! Yeah, sure!" Walter said. He slapped Kenny's shoulder back. "Oh, wait, there's Karen. Karen!" he called and hurried toward her.

"That guy," Kenny said as he and Amanda began to move to the music. "He's something else, huh?"

"He is," Amanda agreed, "something else."

MAGGIE TWOHILL has already written four funny books about middle-grade school kids: *Bigmouth; Jeeter, Mason and the Magic Headset; Superbowl Upset;* and *Who Has the Lucky-Duck in Class 4-B?*

She lives in South Salem, New York.